Lulu  and Bob

For Mum, Dad and James ~
LK

First published in 2011
by Scholastic Children's Books
Euston House, 24 Eversholt Street
London NW1 1DB
a division of Scholastic Ltd
www.scholastic.co.uk

London ~ New York ~ Toronto ~ Sydney ~ Auckland
Mexico City ~ New Delhi ~ Hong Kong

Text and illustrations copyright © 2011 Lerryn Korda

HB ISBN 978 1 407110 02 8
PB ISBN 978 1 407110 04 2

1 3 5 7 9 10 8 6 4 2

(No cats were harmed in the making of this book.)

Lulu and Bob

Lerryn Korda

SCHOLASTIC

This is Lulu. She lives in a lovely house with her mummy, her daddy and Percy the cat.

There are a lot of terribly important things that Lulu is supposed to do.

Lulu's Terribly
Important Things
She must:
tidy up,
put everything back
where it belongs,
brush her hair,
blow her nose
(but not too loudly),
and use her knife and
fork properly.

Most of all, Lulu is supposed to be
a good girl and that means
being on her

very best behaviour,

all the time.

There are also a lot of terribly important things that Lulu is not supposed to do.

She is not supposed to bother Percy,

play ball indoors,

or get messy, muddy or mucky.

She is not supposed to draw anywhere except on the paper.

or leave footprints on the floor.

There is a lot to remember.

And sometimes Lulu just wants to do something different.

Lately, Lulu has noticed that strange things have started to happen.

Lulu wonders what is going on.
Then, one day...

. . . Bob appears.

"Hello! I'm Bob," says Bob.

"Would you like to have some fun?" he asks Lulu.

"It's terribly important, you know."

Bob is an **unusual** sort of person.

He is **very interested** in dressing up.

He likes to have parties.

He especially enjoys chatting.

Lulu thinks she is going to like Bob very much indeed.

On rainy days, Lulu and Bob are really ever so busy.

They have to build houses,

climb mountains

and escape from strange creatures.

"Bob is very brave!" says Lulu.

But there's never any time to tidy up, because there's ever so much to do.

"Bob is rather messy!"
shrugs Lulu.

Today Lulu and Bob are
busy in the beauty parlour.

"Pass the nail varnish!" says Bob.
"Pass the lotion!" says Lulu.
"And now a bit of powder!"
says Bob.

Lulu and Bob are having
a very good time indeed.

But then it all goes
extremely
wrong.

Oh dear!

"Bob was **very naughty!**" says Lulu.

But Bob is nowhere to be found.

Lulu has to sit on the thinking chair.
She thinks for a long time.

"I'm sorry," says Lulu.
"Me too," says Bob.

Then it's time to clean
up the mess.

"Cleaning up is
terribly important!"
says Lulu.

Bob helps.
He actually quite
likes cleaning.

Now Lulu and Bob need cleaning up too.

But at bath time Bob doesn't feel so brave.
Bob is frightened of going down the plughole.

"Don't worry, Bob!" says Lulu.
"Bathtime is fun.
I'll keep you safe."

Soon they are all clean again.
No more mess,
no more muck.

Lulu and Bob are ready for bed at last.

"I hope you'll remember to follow the rules tomorrow," says Lulu. "They're **terribly important** you know!"

"Yes," promises Bob. "I will be on my **very best behavior...**"

"...most of the time."